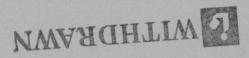

THE LONELY SHADOW

by
Clay Rice

The Lonely Shadow

Published by Familius LLC, Huntsville, Utah, www.familius.com

Familius books are available at special discounts for bulk purchases for sales promotions, family or corporate use. Special editions, including personalized covers, excerpts of existing books, or books with corporate logos, can be created in large quantities for special needs. For more information, contact Premium Sales at 801-552-7298 or email specialmarkets@familius.com

Edited by Pete Wyrick
Book and jacket design by Steve Lepre
Photography by Liz Duren

Printed in China

LCCN: 2012945116

eISBN: 978-1-938301-07-0
pISBN: 978-1-938301-08-7

First Edition

About the Publisher

Familius was founded in 2012 with the intent to align the founders' love of publishing and family with the digital publishing renaissance which occurred simultaneously with the Great Recession. The founders believe that the traditional family is the basic unit of society, and that a society is only as strong as the families that create it.

Familius' mission is to help families be happy. We invite you to participate with us in strengthening your family by being part of the Familius family. Go to www.familius. com to subscribe and receive information about our books, articles, and videos.

Website: www.familius.com
Facebook:www.facebook.com/paterfamilius
Twitter: @paterfamilius1 and @familiustalk
Pinterest: www.pinterest.com/familius

 HELPING FAMILIES BE HAPPY

DEDICATION

To the many children across this country
for whom I've had the pleasure
of creating "shadow pictures"
over the past three decades.

To my wife Caroline; my son Charlie, 3;
and my son Connor, 6, who was the
inspiration and the model for
The Lonely Shadow.

And to my Granddad, who taught me
the art and magic of silhouettes
when I was a little boy.

ACKNOWLEDGEMENTS

To Steve Lepre. Thank you for your
creativity and your genius.

To Katherine Rice who, a long time ago,
told me I could do anything I truly wanted to do.

THE LONELY SHADOW

Early one morning,
a little shadow
stood under a street lamp
and sighed.

"I am very lonely," he thought.

The shadow Knew that he
belonged to someone,
he just didn't Know who.

He thought, "If I could find my mate,
I would be very happy."

The little shadow went for a walk,
and while he walked he sang a song:

*I have no you
you have no me,
you and me
we have no we,
but if I find you
and you find me,
happy we will always be.*

The shadow stood by a door.

Am I a door?

He stood by a chair.

Am I a chair?

The shadow paused by an old man
wearing polka dot underwear.

He looked high and he looked low,
but his mate did not show.

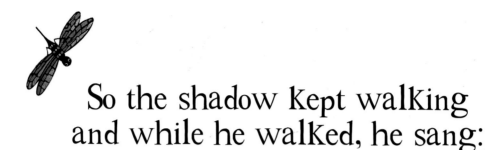

So the shadow Kept walKing
and while he walKed, he sang:

*I have no you
you have no me,
you and me
we have no we,
but if I find you
and you find me,
happy we will always be.*

The little shadow went into the forest.

He dined with a deer.

He drank with a drake.

He stretched himself skinny and snuck wit

snake.

But nowhere could
he find his mate.

He leaned against a tree.
He was very sad.
"If I could find my mate
how happy I would be."

Suddenly, a wise owl appeared.

"Don't be sad, little shadow," he said.
"You are just looking
in the wrong places.
You must go
where the children are."

This made the shadow happy.

He ran...and ran...
until he heard the sound of children
playing on the playground.

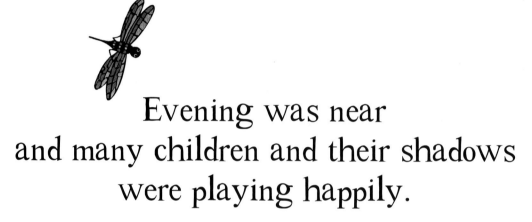

Evening was near
and many children and their shadows
were playing happily.

Then he saw a boy sitting all alone.

The little boy seemed sad.

The shadow walked up to the boy and asked, "Why are you so sad?"

The boy said, "It's late in the day, and that's when all the shadows come out to play. And I don't have one."

"I'll play with you,"
said the shadow.
"All right," said the boy.

They kicked a ball.

They streaked down a slide.

They jumped in a wagon and went for a ride.

They climbed a big tree.

They posed by a lake.

The bullfrog said "ribbit"
as they swam with the drake.

They slipped through the door.

They raced by the chair.

They pulled polka dots from
Grandpa's underwear.

And later that night as the
shadows grew long.

They tooK to the bed
as the big clocK
went gong.

I have you,
you have me.
Together
we will always be.

ABOUT SILHOUETTES

by Clay Rice

More than 250 years ago a
Frenchman named Silhouette
thought it would be fun to cut out
shadow shapes with scissors and
black paper. He cut out shadow pictures
of all of his friends and made cutouts
to give as gifts.

Other artists started making cutouts, too, and
they called them silhouettes after the man
who started the art form.

After all these years, only a few artists
still make silhouette cutouts.

My grandfather, Carew Rice, was a
silhouette artist. When I was a little boy,
I loved watching him create beautiful
picture cutouts. I started doing them, too.
I've been doing them professionally for
more than thirty years.